This book belongs to:

_____

Let Me Read is a series of books ideal for children who are starting to read. It encourages involvement of parents with children. The story can be read out aloud by the parent. The simple text encourages children to join in and the colourful illustrations help to hold their interest. Older children can read the stories by themselves.

Level 1 - Age 5 and above

Level 2 - Age 6 and above

Level 3 - Age 7 and above

Level 4 - Age 8 and above

New Dawn Press
STERLING GROUP
New Dawn Press, Inc., 244 South Randall Rd # 90, Elgin, IL 60123
e-mail: sales@newdawnpress.com

New Dawn Press, 2 Tintern Close, Slough, Berkshire, SL1-2TB, UK
e-mail: ndpuk@newdawnpress.com
sterlingdis@yahoo.co.uk

Sterling Publishers (P) Ltd.
A-59, Okhla Industrial Area, Phase-II, New Delhi-110020
e-mail: sterlingpublishers@airtelbroadband.in
ghai@nde.vsnl.net.in

Sterling Publishers Ltd. C/o Minerva Fiduciary Services (Mauritius) Limited
Suite 2004, Level 2, Alexander House, 35 Cybercity, Ebene, Mauritius
Tel: (230) 464 5100 Fax: (230) 464 3100
e-mail: uttamg@minerva.my

Let Me Read

The Ugly Duckling

Mamma Duck was very excited. The eggs she was sitting on were about to hatch. Soon she would have seven little ducklings.

One fine day the eggs hatched. The little babies came out one by one.

The forest was filled with the quack quack of seven hungry ducklings.

Mamma Duck wiped their feathers and got them all in line. She stood looking at her family proudly.

When she looked at the last
one, she said, "Why, you are
ugly! The egg you came
from must have rolled into
my nest by mistake.
Go away, you are not
my baby."

The poor little duckling
walked away sadly.

He walked and he walked
till he came to a large farm.

On the farm he saw a turkey.

"Are you my mother?" asked the poor little duckling.

"No, I'm not. You are so ugly! Go away."

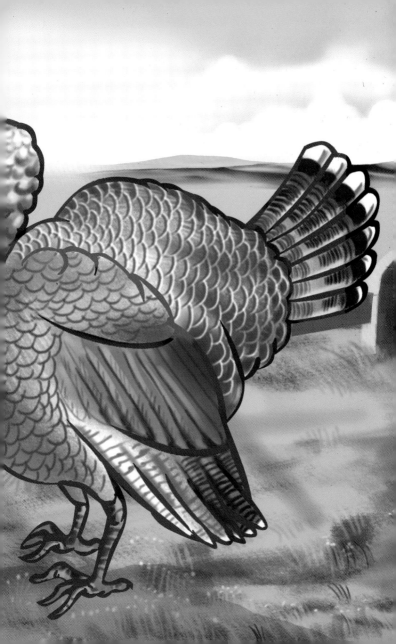

The poor duckling walked away. He soon saw a hen with her little chicks.

"Have you lost a baby?" asked the duckling.

"No, my babies are all here," said the hen.

The sad little duckling
walked away.

He then met a peacock.

"Am I your baby?" asked the
little duckling.

"How can you be my baby?
You do not have beautiful
feathers like mine," said
the peacock.

He next met a macaw. Its feathers were red, blue, green and yellow.

"Are you my mother?" asked the sad duckling.

"Don't be silly!" said the macaw and told him to run along.

As he walked away, he met a cow.

"Are you my mother?" he asked her.

"Do I look like your mother?" laughed the cow.

The poor little duckling was tired and sad.

As he walked on, he reached a pool and saw his reflection in the water. "How ugly I am!" he said.

"There you are, my poor lost baby!" said a swan standing nearby. "You are not ugly.

You are the most beautiful baby in the world. And when you grow up, you will be a beautiful swan."

How many ducklings did Mamma Duck have?

What did the cow say to the sad duckling?